—The—
as Story

Long, long ago, the emperor of Rome, Caesar Augustus, ordered the people of the empire to the cities of their ancestors to be counted.

To obey this command, a carpenter named Joseph and his wife Mary had to travel from their home in Nazareth to Bethlehem, the city of Joseph's ancestors. Bethlehem was in a country called Judea.

Mary was going to have a baby. She and Joseph knew that the baby would be the Son of God because an angel had appeared and told them that God had chosen Mary to be the mother of His child. The angel said that the baby's name would be Jesus.

When Mary and Joseph arrived in Bethlehem, it was almost dark. The town was already crowded with people who had come to be counted.

Mary and Joseph tried to find a place to stay, but all the inns were full. Joseph began to worry, but then an innkeeper offered to help.

"I have no room in my inn, but I do have a stable in the back," he said. "You can sleep there if you like, although you'll have to share it with the animals. Still, there is plenty of clean hay on the floor, so you should be comfortable."

Mary looked around at the animals inside the stable and saw that they were gentle and kind. She remembered the message that God's angel had given her, and she knew that everything would be all right.

"Your baby will be born a holy king and his kingdom will last forever," the angel had said.

"I know that God will look after us wherever we are," Mary said to Joseph.

That night Mary's baby was born. She wrapped him warmly and laid him in a manger filled with soft hay.

The animals gathered around to keep the tiny new baby safe as he slept. They knew that he was the Son of God and they all loved him.

On the night Jesus was born, there were some shepherds in a field near Bethlehem, looking after their sheep.

As they looked up into the night sky, an angel suddenly appeared with light shining brightly all around.

At first the shepherds were scared, but the angel spoke kindly to them.

"Don't be afraid," the angel said. "I have come to tell you some joyful news. Today a savior has been born in Bethlehem. You will find him in a stable, lying in a manger."

Then the sky was filled with more angels, all singing God's praises.

"We must find this wonderful baby!" cried the shepherds. So off they went, carrying the smallest lambs in their arms.

The shepherds hurried to Bethlehem and found the stable. When they looked inside, they saw the Baby Jesus in the manger, just as the angel had said.

"It's true!" they cried. "The Son of God is born!" They knelt down to worship the baby and they offered their little lambs as gifts.

Far away in the East, three wise men were watching the night sky when they saw a bright new star appear.

"This star is the sign we have been waiting for," they said. "The Son of God has been born. We must find him and worship him."

The three wise men saddled their camels and journeyed over mountains and deserts. They carried beautiful gold and silver boxes covered with jewels. The boxes held gifts of gold and richly scented ointments called frankincense and myrrh.

The wise men followed the brilliant new star to Bethlehem. Finally the star stopped right above the stable.

"This must be the place we've been looking for," the wise men said. Softly, they pushed the door open.

Inside, the animals were completely quiet and still. They did not want to wake the Baby Jesus, who lay fast asleep in his mother's arms.

"At last our long journey is over," the wise men whispered. "The star has led us to the Son of God."

They knelt down and prayed to the holy baby. Then, one by one, they opened the boxes and laid their gifts in the soft, clean straw at the feet of the Baby Jesus.

The three wise men knew that they had seen the savior of the world.

But not everyone was happy about the birth of the Baby Jesus. When Herod, the king of Judea, heard people say a new king was born, he was very angry. He didn't want any other king in his land.

"Find this baby everyone is talking about," he shouted to his soldiers. "And then I want you to kill him!"

That night an angel came to Joseph in his dreams and warned him to take his family somewhere far away so they would be safe. Joseph and Mary took their child and fled into Egypt. When Herod's soldiers searched Bethlehem, the Baby Jesus was gone.

As Jesus grew up, he taught many people about God's love. People all over the world still believe in what he said, and every Christmas they celebrate the birth of the little baby in Bethlehem.